Winnie & Ernst

Gina Freschet

Farrar Straus Giroux
New York

For my good friends Bob and Sally

Copyright © 2003 by Gina Freschet
All rights reserved
Distributed in Canada by Douglas & McIntyre Ltd.
Color separations by Chroma Graphics PTE Ltd.
Printed and bound in the United States of America
by Phoenix Color Corporation
Typography by Jennifer Crilly
First edition, 2003
1 3 5 7 9 10 8 6 4 2

Library of Congress Cataloging-in-Publication Data
Freschet, Gina.
    Winnie and Ernst / Gina Freschet.— 1st ed.
        p.   cm.
    Summary: Winnie the possum and Ernst the otter go to a birthday
party, bake for a bake sale, hold a garden party, and turn bad luck
into good luck.
    ISBN 0-374-38452-5
    [1. Friendship—Fiction. 2. Opossums—Fiction. 3. Otters—
Fiction. 4. Animals—Fiction.] I. Title.

PZ7.F889685 Wi 2003
[E]—dc21
                                                    2002023161

Contents

Winnie and Ernst Go Hunting

It was the day of Ms. Zora Beaver's birthday party. Ernst knocked on Winnie's door. It flew open.

"I'm not ready!" Winnie cried, and pulled Ernst inside. "I can't find the gift! I've lost it!"

"Where did you leave it?" asked Ernst.

"If I knew that," said Winnie, "it wouldn't be lost. Help me look," she pleaded.

They hunted through her house. Ernst went
to the kitchen. He looked in the cupboards.
He looked in the Mixmaster. He looked in the
refrigerator and got himself a snack.

"Wait a minute. What am I looking for?"

Winnie said, "You are looking for Ms. Zora
Beaver's birthday present!"

"Is it a bug?" asked
Ernst. "There's a bug in
the blender."
"No," said Winnie.

"Is it a banana peel?
There's a banana peel in
the fruit bowl."
But Winnie said, "No,
it isn't a banana peel."

"Did you get her
cobwebs? There's
cobwebs on the tea set."
Winnie said, "Are you
looking or what?"
"Well," said Ernst,
"how will I know it
when I find it?"

Winnie told Ernst, "It's a mood ring. It has a stone that changes colors when you're happy or sad. It's in a little blue box."

She tapped her chin. "I wonder if I hid it in a pocket."

She went to the closet and threw down all her clothes and costumes. She searched all the pockets. No dice.

"We have to find it," whined Winnie. "We can't go to the party without a gift."

"I have a gift," said Ernst. "It can be from both of us."

"What is it?"

"It's a surprise."

"Is it a pair of skates?" Winnie asked.

"No, it's not skates."

"Is it a Fishin' Musician? Soap on a rope?"

"Nope."

"An ant farm? A Lava lamp? Sea-Monkeys?"

Ernst shook his head until Winnie demanded, "What is it?!"

"It's a pinecone," said Ernst. "A perfect pinecone."

Winnie just looked at him. "What for?"

"I don't know. But I'm sure it will be useful for something."

Winnie said, "Let's keep looking."

Ernst looked in the fish-head soup tureen.
He looked in Winnie's silkworm box, in her
bowling-ball bag, and behind all the pictures of
Winnie having lunch.

Together, all they found was an old dog
biscuit, a fuzzy lollipop, and Winnie's missing
copy of *Cooking with Smoke and Mirrors*.

11

"Aha!" said Winnie. She went to her bookcase and took out all her books.

"Aha!" she said again, because there, behind the very last book of Eskimo campfire songs, was the blue box. Winnie eagerly opened it.

"Oh no!" Winnie wailed. The box was empty. "Where can it be?" She clapped her paws to her face.

"Right under your nose," said Ernst. He pointed to her paw. On it was a sparkling red ring.

Winnie laughed. "Now I remember! I put it on so I wouldn't lose it!" She let out a big sigh, and the mood ring instantly changed to milky blue. Winnie put it back in its box.

At Ms. Zora Beaver's house, there were
balloons and games and prizes and music.

Ms. Beaver got a pair of goggles and a
Frisbee and a bracelet and a necklace. And
a mood ring.

Plus, she got a perfect pinecone, which turned out to be a perfect jewelry tree.

Winnie and Ernst's Nut Loaf

It was early morning, and the big bake sale was that afternoon. Winnie and Ernst still couldn't decide what to bake.

"How about a coconut cream pie?" said Ernst.

"Look around," said Winnie. "Do you see any coconut trees?"

"How about a cake?"

"Boring," said Winnie. "*Everyone* will bring a cake."

They thought and thought until Winnie finally said, "I know! We'll make my Aunt Sally's Famous Nut Loaf."

"What's it famous for?" asked Ernst.

"For selling at bake sales."

Winnie and Ernst got out some butter, eggs, sugar, flour, apples, spices, berries, salt, and baking powder. They mixed it all up and poured it in a pan and baked it in the oven.

When the loaf came out, it was golden brown and puffy and fluffy.

On the way to the bake sale, they met Wally.
Winnie said, "Would you like to sample my
Aunt Sally's Famous Nut Loaf?"

"Glad to," said the rabbit. He took a nibble.
"Not bad," said Wally. "But something seems
to be missing."

Next Webber hopped by. Winnie offered him
some of Aunt Sally's Famous Nut Loaf, too.
He took a slurp and said, "It's all right, but I
doubt it will sell at the bake sale."

"Why not?" said Winnie.

Two field mice came along. They took a taste, and both made a face. "Something's missing," they said.

"But what is it?" wailed Winnie. "Vanilla?"

"Nooo," burped Webber.

"Honey?" asked Ernst.

"Nooo," said Wally.

"Raisins!" the field mice blurted out.

"Yes! Yes!" everyone shouted. "It needs raisins!"

Winnie huffed. "There aren't any raisins in the recipe!"

All of them shook their heads regretfully. They left Winnie and Ernst and went on their way to the bake sale.

Winnie looked sadly at her last little piece of Aunt Sally's Famous Nut Loaf.

"Don't listen to them," said Ernst. "Rabbits eat grass, frogs eat flies, and mice will eat anything. What do they know about fine baking?"

"I know one thing." Winnie sniffled. "Aunt Sally's Famous Nut Loaf isn't very famous after all."

Just then Watson came by. Winnie gave him the last piece of the not-so-famous nut loaf.

"Delicious," said Watson. "Except for one thing: no nuts."

"No nuts?!" cried Winnie.

"No nuts?!" said Ernst. "No nuts in the nut loaf! The Famous Nutless Nut Loaf!" He laughed himself silly until Winnie was laughing, too.

"Follow me," said Watson.

He took Winnie and Ernst to all of his secret
hiding places. Under logs, roots, and rocks they
found walnuts, chestnuts, pine nuts, and more
acorns than you could shake a stick at.

Winnie and Ernst gathered all they could
carry. They thanked Watson and hurried back
to Winnie's kitchen, where they made another
loaf—this time with plenty of nuts.

It was just as golden brown and puffy and
fluffy as the first one—only nuttier.

At the bake sale, it became known as Winnie and Ernst's Famous Nut Loaf. They sold every crunchy, munchy piece and gave most of their earnings to the local home for lost loons.

There was enough left over to buy Watson a bag of walnuts to last him all winter.

Winnie's Garden Party

The long, cold winter was ending. Winnie looked out her window. She saw the first flower in her yard. It was yellow. After months of gray skies and white snow, it made her very happy.

"I'll have a garden party," she said, "on the first day of spring." She checked her calendar. The first day of spring was in just one week. She had to get busy and send out invitations.

She would invite Wally and Webber and Old Thorny the turtle, and the ducks, Ling and Ing. And of course the Buttress Badgers. She asked Ernst to come over and help. "What should I say?" asked Winnie, tapping the pen on her tiny teeth.

"How about this?" Ernst said.

"Perfect!" said Winnie.

Replies came the next day by Post Owl Service. Winnie was delighted. "So *everyone* is coming to my garden party!"

First Winnie and Ernst tackled the garden. They shoveled the last of the snow, cracked the ice in the birdbath, and painted all the lawn chairs different colors.

Then they began to cook. The good smells brought some of the young guests early, and Ernst had to shoo them away. "The party is tomorrow," he told them.

That night, Winnie could hardly sleep. In her dream, snow began falling. The way it falls in a snow globe. Silently.

When Winnie woke up, she went to the window and pulled back the curtains. *"Eek!"* she screamed.

Her yard was knee-deep in snow. There was no yellow flower, nothing but white snow and gray sky.

Ernst came by early to start the flapjacks. He found Winnie crying. "The party is wrecked! Whoever heard of a blizzard on the first day of spring? Whoever heard of a garden party in the snow?"

Ernst said, "Well, you know our neighbors. I bet they're still coming. There's free food."

"Of course they're still coming!" Winnie said. "What should we do?"

"Whatever it is, we'd better do it fast," said Ernst.

He went outside and brought in all the lawn chairs. Next he and Winnie dragged in all the porch plants.

Winnie quickly got her arts-and-crafts kit of paper, glue, paints, and glitter.

"Here, take this end," she told Ernst, and they strung green garlands all around the room.

"Hurry," said Winnie. She and Ernst twisted up dozens of paper flowers and tied them to the bare bushes.

Winnie sprayed her favorite perfume, Mink Stink, around the room. The doorbell rang, and she jumped.

The raccoons were the first to arrive. Right away they went to wash their hands.

The doorbell rang again. It was Mrs. Buttress Badger. She was very hard to please, and, to begin with, her feet were wet.

But when she stepped inside, Mrs. Buttress Badger proclaimed, "What a beautiful indoor garden!"

Next came Wally the rabbit with his entire
family, then Webber the frog, Old Thorny, and
Ling and Ing. Ernst handed out sunglasses.
They all shook the snow off and stepped into
Winnie's new indoor-garden parlor.

When the robins made a surprise appearance
and began singing, the scene was complete.
It felt just like spring.

Winnie and Ernst Have Luck

One spring day, Ernst was waiting for Winnie to come home. He looked up at the trees and saw something sparkly there.

"What's that?" he wondered.

"It's me." Zack, a blackbird, flew down. In one claw he clutched a piece of tin. It winked in the sunshine. "I'm practicing my flash signals," said Zack, "so I can talk to my distant cousin Jay."

"Can I try?" said Ernst.

"Sure. Do you have any foil?"

"No," said Ernst.

"Not even a gum wrapper?"

"No."

"How about a mirror?"

"Yes!" said Ernst, and he ran into the house and got Winnie's mirror.

But when he ran back out, he tripped. The mirror fell and smashed into pieces.

"Oops," said Zack. "Bad luck, pal. *Seven years'* bad luck." He cackled and flew away.

Ernst looked at the broken mirror at his feet. What would he tell Winnie? She was sure to be mad. She really liked her mirror.

Ernst had a brainstorm. He took the mirror into the house. He glued it back together.

Then he got Winnie's paints. Quickly he painted a picture of Winnie's face on the cracked mirror. He thought it looked exactly like her.

He finished just in time. Winnie waltzed through the door.

"Tada!" she sang when she saw Ernst. She struck a pose. "How do you like my new hat?"

Ernst said, "It's hard to tell."

Winnie swept her mirror off the table to look and . . .

"*Eek!*" she shrieked. She dropped the mirror, and it smashed again.

"Oh no!" cried Winnie. "Bad luck!" She put her paws on her bare head and screeched again. "Where's my new hat? Seven years' bad luck, and it has started already. I've lost my new hat."

She ran to the kitchen and threw salt over her shoulder.

She turned around three times and hopped on one foot. She walked backwards and did a flip.

She spit in her paw and said, "Hookity, hookity, Betty Boopity. There, that should cancel the bad luck."

Ernst hung his head and admitted, "It's my fault. I broke your mirror first, and you broke it next."

"Quick!" said Winnie. She threw salt over his shoulder and spun him around three times and made him hop on one foot and walk backwards and do a flip and spit in his paw and say, "Hookity, hookity, Betty Boopity."

"Now," said Ernst, "let's look for your hat."
They went back to all the places where
Winnie had walked on her way home.

They looked in the bushes. Winnie got stuck
by the stickers. "Ouch," she said. "Bad luck."

Ernst tore his jacket on a branch. "More bad
luck," Winnie observed.

When they looked near the pond, Winnie
lost her shoe in the muck. "Yet more bad
luck!" she shouted.

It was getting dark. "This is awful," said
Winnie. "Now I've lost my hat *and* my shoe.
And you have torn your jacket." She was just
about to give up when they heard the lovely
song of a wood thrush.

Winnie and Ernst followed the sound. Under a holly tree was the thrush, happily building her nest. Building her nest in Winnie's new hat!

Winnie said, "Excuse me, but that's my new hat."

"Is it?" said the thrush. "Oh dear. It would have made a perfect home for my children."

Winnie bravely sighed and said, "Never mind. You keep it. It's just my bad luck."

Ernst whisked off his porkpie hat. He offered it to the thrush instead.

"Oh," she chirped, "this will make an even better home."

And it did.

Winnie plucked the twigs out of her hat and put it on. It looked very becoming indeed.

"See?" said Ernst. "We have turned bad luck into good luck."

And Winnie had to agree.